This book belongs to

....

This is the story of Gingerbread Fred.

You can read it in a chair, or read it in bed,

You can get someone else to read it instead!

There's something else. Can you guess what?

On every page there's a mouse to spot!

This edition first published in 2011 by Castle Street Press
an imprint of make believe ideas ltd.

Text copyright © 2006 Nick and Claire Page
Copyright © 2006 make believe ideas ltd.
The Wilderness, Berkhamsted, Hertfordshire, HP4 2AZ, UK.
565 Royal Parkway, Nashville, TI 37214, USA.

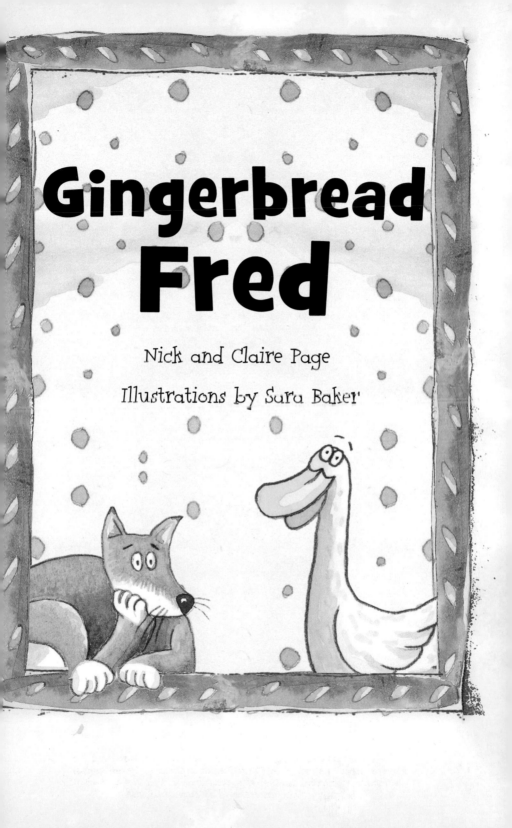

Gingerbread
Fred

Nick and Claire Page

Illustrations by Sara Baker

There once was a little old baker
and a little old baker's wife.
One day, they baked a gingerbread
man who magically came to life!

The name that they gave him was
Gingerbread Fred. They said to him:
"Don't go out on the street! You are
not a real boy, you're a cookie, and
that makes you yummy to eat!"

But before you could say
"JELLY DOUGHNUTS,"
their gingerbread son
had started to run!

And Gingerbread Fred said...

8

"Run, run, run,
as fast as you can.
You can't catch me,
I'm the gingerbread man!"

First, Gingerbread Fred reached a garden
where a cat lay asleep in the flowers.
"MEE-WOW!" said the cat.
"Here comes breakfast!
I've been waiting for hours and hours!"

But Fred didn't wait –
he started to skate!

And Gingerbread Fred said...

"Skate, skate, skate,
as fast as you can.
You can't catch me,
I'm the gingerbread man!"

13

Next, Gingerbread Fred reached a farmyard
where a dog was lying about.
"BOW-WOW!" said the dog.
"It must be lunchtime!
It's a gingerbread man takeout!"

But before you could say,
"LEMON CHEESECAKE,"
Fred turned aside
and started to ride!

And Gingerbread Fred said...

"Ride, ride, ride,
as fast as you can.
You can't catch me,
I'm the gingerbread man!"

Then Gingerbread Fred reached the river
where a fox sat, watching the fish.
"Need some help?" said the fox.
"Jump on my back.
I can take you across, if you wish."

Fred grabbed his coat
and the fox was a boat!

And Gingerbread Fred said...

"Swim, swim, swim,
as fast as you can.
You can't catch me,
I'm the gingerbread man!"

As the water gradually rose,
the fox said to Fred:
"Move up further.
It's best if you sit on my nose."

Quite soon, they were over the river,
and Gingerbread Fred said: "Good-bye!"
"Not so fast," said the fox.
"There's one more thing.
Now, how would you like to fly?"

And before you could say
"GINGER SNAPS,"
Fred was thrown high up in the sky!

And Gingerbread Fred said...

24

"Fly fly, fly,
as fast as you can.
You can't catch me,
I'm the…"

CRUNCH! SCRUNCH! MUNCH!
The fox had him for lunch.

And Gingerbread Fred said
nothing ever again.

Ready to tell

Oh no! Some of the pictures from this story have been mixed up! Can you retell the story and point to each picture in the correct order?

Picture dictionary

Encourage your child to read these harder words from the story and gradually develop their basic vocabulary.

baker   breakfast   fish

gingerbread man   ride   river

run   skate   wife

Key words

Here are some key words used in context.
Help your child to use other words
from the border in simple sentences.

There **was** a little old baker.

They baked **a** gingerbread man.

"Fly as fast as you **can.**"

The **dog** saw Gingerbread Fred.

"**Get** on my back."

a • he • is • said • go • you • are • this • going • they • away • play • cat • to

Bake Gingerbread Fred

Ask a grown-up to help you bake Fred and his friends.
You can eat them if they look like they're running away.

You will need

4 oz butter • 3 tbsp golden molasses • 1½ cups self-
raising flour • ready-made icing in a tube • 1–2 tsp
ground ginger • ½ cup superfine sugar • 1 egg, beaten
• saucepan • mixing bowl • large spoon • greased
baking sheet • a gingerbread-man cutter • colored
chocolate beans

What to do

1 Turn the oven on to 350°F.
2 Melt the butter and molasses in a pan over a gentle heat.
3 Put the flour, ginger and sugar in a mixing bowl.
Add the melted butter and molasses, stir in slightly and
then add the egg.
4 Mix the ingredients together until smooth and then
leave for 15 minutes to cool.
5 Roll out to a thickness of ¼ inch and use the cutter
to cut out the Gingerbread Fred shapes.
6 Place on a the baking sheet and cook in the middle
of the oven for about eight minutes, or until golden
brown. Remove and leave to cool.
7 Decorate with icing eyes and mouth, and make buttons
from colored chocolate beans stuck on with a spot of icing.